The Pooka Party

Shona Shirley Macdonald

℗

THE O'BRIEN PRESS
DUBLIN

Now listen very carefully, I'm going to tell you about a magical creature called ...

the Pooka!

It's a shapeshifter,

which means it can take the shape of a goat ...

a dog

a cat

an eagle

a horse

a snail

or even a person!

a hare

It likes living alone
in the mountains,
where it spends its time ...

6

fixing things,

making soup,

painting, singing, gardening and dancing

(all at the same time).

But one day, suddenly these things were not fun anymore.

The Pooka was lonely.
It hadn't seen its friends in ages.

So it turned itself into a snail

and hid away for a long time ...
until it had an idea.

Why not have a party?

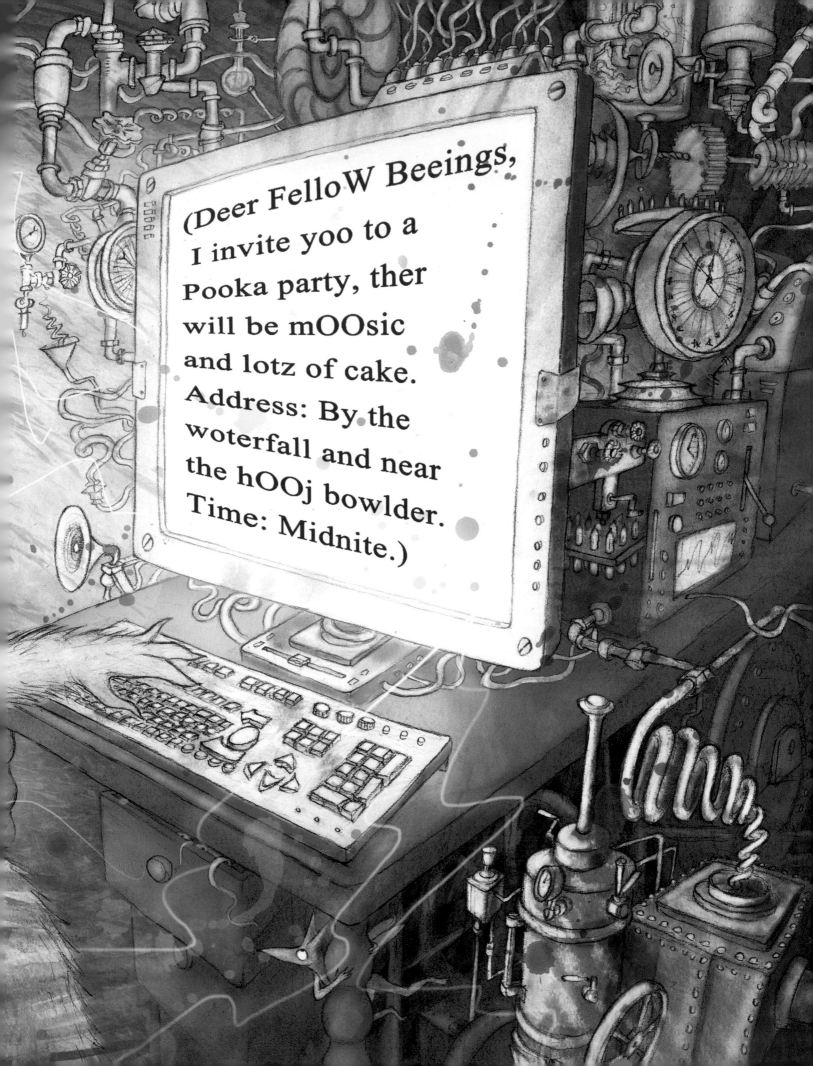

The Pooka baked cakes,

put up decorations,

combed its beard

and waited ...

and waited ...

and waited ...

but no one came.

The Pooka was so sad and tired that it curled up ...

and went to sleep.

So it didn't hear the door creeeeaaaaking open.

Everyone had come after all!

Soon they were so busy chatting
and playing music

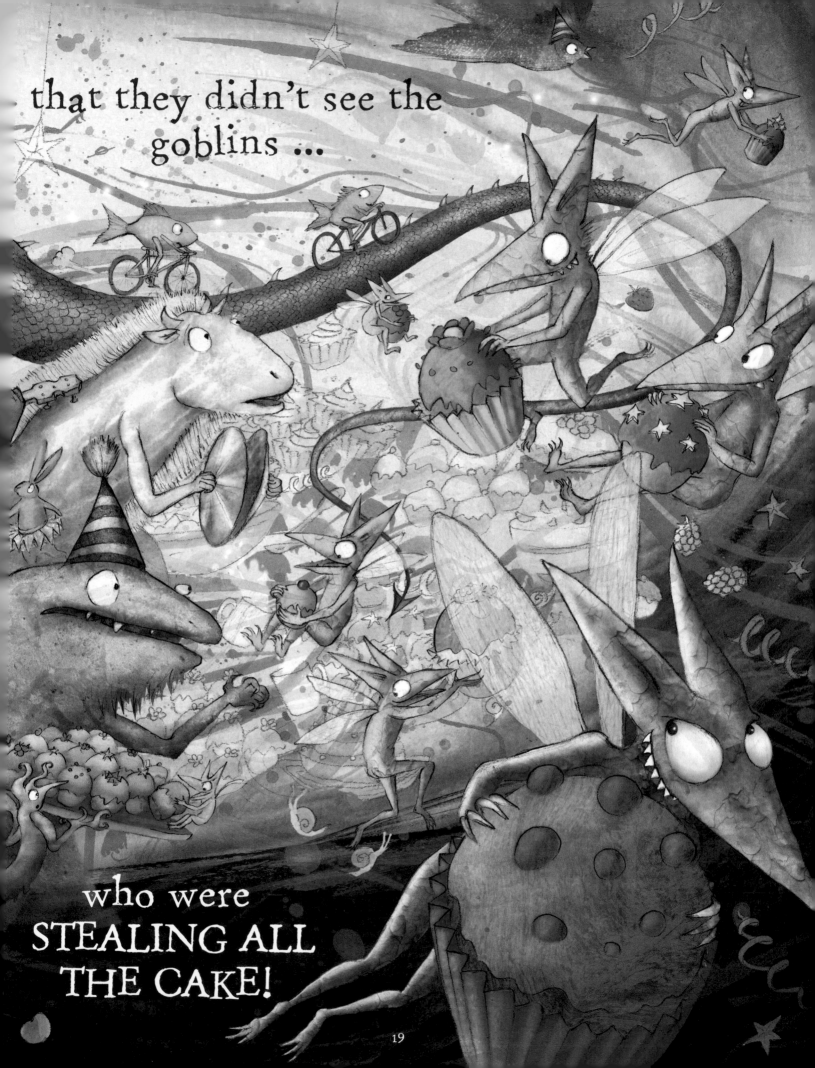

that they didn't see the goblins ...

who were
STEALING ALL
THE CAKE!

'After them!' cried the Pooka.

Everyone dashed outside and tried to catch the goblins.

But instead it turned into a
MIGHTY CAKE BATTLE!

It got so noisy that they woke up the Moon,

who was not happy.

The Moon made the goblins say sorry. And they all went back to the Pooka's house,

where the Pooka gave
them delicious, sparkly soup.

The goblins too – as long as they promised to be good.

When the party was over,
everyone flew,
scampered or
galloped home,

and the Pooka fell asleep.
It wasn't lonely anymore.
(It was busy planning the next party!)

Shona Shirley Macdonald is an award-winning illustrator/author, originally from Scotland and now living by the sea in County Waterford. Her other illustrated titles include *An Féileacán agus an Rí* written by Máire Zepf, which won the Gradam Réics Carló (Book of the Year for Young Readers), and *The Moon Spun Round: W.B. Yeats for Children*, edited by Noreen Doody. She has also exhibited her work throughout Ireland in both solo and group shows, and internationally at the Bratislava Illustration Biennial. *The Pooka Party* was chosen for the 2020 IBBY (International Board on Books for Young People) Honor List and shortlisted for the Irish Book Awards 2018 – Children's Book of the Year (Junior), and the Children's Books Ireland Book of the Year 2019.

'Mysterious and beautiful illustrations spin out from Yeats's haunting and enchanted words and rhythms, bringing the spirit and beauty of his writing in this collection to a whole new audience.'
Primary Times

'Gossamer-light drawings dance around the text like a wave on the sea … will enchant readers of all ages and open many eyes to the beauty of the poetry.'
Evening Echo

'Absolutely gorgeous.'
Eithne Shortall, *Sunday Times*

'Faery worlds and faery creatures come to life through the colourful illustrations and will instantly appeal to children.'
Seomra Ranga

First published 2021 by The O'Brien Press Ltd,
12 Terenure Road East, Rathgar, Dublin 6, D06 HD27, Ireland
Tel: +353 1 4923333; Fax: +353 1 4922777
E-mail: books@obrien.ie
Website: www.obrien.ie
First published in hardback 2018
The O'Brien Press is a member of Publishing Ireland.

ISBN: 978-1-78849-277-5

6 5 4 3 2 1
23 22 21

Printed and bound by Gutenberg Press, Malta.
The paper in this book is produced using pulp from managed forests.

Published in

DUBLIN
UNESCO
City of Literature